R6767a

And the Winner Is...

And the Winner Is...

by Stephen Roos

Illustrated by Dee deRosa

Atheneum   1989   New York

Atheneum
Macmillan Publishing Company
866 Third Avenue, New York, NY 10022
Collier Macmillan Canada, Inc.
First Edition   Printed in the United States of America
10   9   8   7   6   5   4   3   2   1

Library of Congress Cataloging-in-Publication Data
Roos, Stephen.
And the winner is . . ./by Stephen Roos;
illustrated by Dee deRosa.   p.   cm.
Summary: Distraught over her family's financial state,
which is forcing them to sell their vacation home on the
island where they spend each summer, twelve-year-old
Phoebe sees her close friendship with Kit self-destructing as
they both become involved in a local talent show.
ISBN 0–689–31300–4
[1. Friendship—Fiction.   2. Contests—Fiction.   3. Islands—
Fiction.]   I. DeRosa, Dee, ill.   II. Title.
PZ7.R6753An   1989   [Fic]—dc19   88-27519   CIP   AC

For
ALICE KRAUSE
and
SALLY COWAN

And the Winner Is...

1

EVEN BEFORE PHOEBE wiped the sleep from her eyes, she remembered it all over again. Every night for a month now she had prayed for the memory to take a day off and leave her alone. But every morning it was back, waiting for her.

Wearily she got out of bed and stepped to the window. Once upon a time she had taken a definite delight in snapping the shade to the top of the frame and greeting another glorious Plymouth Island day. But "once upon a time" had ended four weeks, two days, and thirteen hours ago. Nothing in Phoebe's world was very definite anymore.

Phoebe gazed at the rose garden her mother had planted their first summer in the house. Beyond the garden were the dark green lawns that led to the bluff. Beyond the bluff was the Atlantic Ocean. As Phoebe opened the window, she heard the waves crash along the shore and smelled the salt in the air.

The sun was well along its ascent in a perfectly blue sky, but Phoebe knew the sun wouldn't reach quite so high today as it had the day before. It was September, and summer was practically over. Soon it would be time for Phoebe to leave the island, as she did at the end of every summer. This time, however, Phoebe would be leaving forever.

August had begun frantically. The phone rang through the day and sometimes into the night and messengers arrived at all hours to deliver ominous-looking envelopes and take more away. Phoebe's father had holed himself up by the phone in the den, coming out only for meals, looking anxious, sometimes snapping at Phoebe or her mother and then apologizing for acting that way.

Her father's business in Philadelphia was in deep trouble. Two major deals had fallen through and Mr. Wilson needed cash, lots of it and right away, to keep the firm afloat. The problems were as complicated as they were urgent, and Phoebe figured the less she knew about them the sooner they would go away. But her father looked so angry and her mother looked so brave that Phoebe couldn't help worrying.

She tried not to fear the worst. She tried not to imagine what the worst could mean. Then one day the phones stopped ringing and the messengers stopped arriving. It was over at last.

Her mother and father had asked her to walk on the beach and watch the sunset with them. As the wind from the Atlantic whipped around them, her dad explained what had gone on at his firm. "Setback" was the word he used. Phoebe was relieved he hadn't described it as either a calamity or a catastrophe.

From now on the Wilsons would have to economize, he told her. Two of the cars, the Lincoln and the BMW convertible, would be sold. The cook and the gardener in Philadelphia would be let go. Violet, their maid, would stay. But until things got better, there would be no more skiing in Utah or sight-seeing in Europe or shopping sprees anywhere.

"Then things will be the way they've always been?" Phoebe asked. "Just less of it?"

"Almost," her mother said. She was looking brave again, which made Phoebe apprehensive.

"But not quite," her father said. "We won't be coming back to Plymouth Island next summer."

"We *always* come back," Phoebe protested. "It's where we belong."

Her mother put her arm around Phoebe's shoulders and held her close. "We're going to have to sell the house here," she said, so softly that her voice was almost a whisper. "We did everything we could to find another way. We need the cash and there isn't anything else to sell that hasn't been sold already."

Phoebe pulled away abruptly. She was frightened by her mother's words and at the same time certain she had not heard her mother correctly. "It's not our house anymore?" she asked.

"For now," her father said. "But not for long."

"When do they move in?" Phoebe asked angrily, not knowing or caring who they were but hating them even so.

"We'll put the house on the market in September," her mother said. "It will be shown but it probably won't be sold until after we're back home and you're in school. Dad and I are going to Philadelphia, Phoebe. We're going to spend the rest of the summer reorganizing the firm. We'll be back for a bit in September so that we can all say good-bye to the house together. We want you to stay here with Violet and have as much fun as you can, right up to the end."

Phoebe felt something like a sob well up in her throat. "Fun?" she asked. "When I'll never be coming back to the island? Never be coming back to this house? What am I supposed to tell my friends?"

"Can you give it a try, honey?" her father asked. "You have wonderful friends here. They'll understand. They'll help."

Phoebe said nothing. She saw the hurt in her father's and mother's eyes. They loved Plymouth as much as she did, loved every inch of the old house as much as she did. She couldn't tell them they were asking her to do the impossible.

Even if there had been words for how Phoebe felt, her voice would have been too faint to be heard above the crashing waves. Her parents had no words either. Silently Phoebe took her father's hand and then her mother's, and the three of them headed up the stairs along the bluff together.

After her parents had left for Philadelphia, Phoebe had talked with Violet a lot and cried a lot with her, too. But she had put off telling her friends. Saying good-bye to them was as impossible as saying good-bye to the island. Telling them the truth about what had happened was even harder. What would they think about her family's misfortune? So she pretended everything was as it had always been. But now the pretending was getting harder. Today Phoebe wondered if it would be easier if she didn't see her friends at all.

She sat down at the white wicker dressing table and pushed the silver-plated brush through her shoulder-length black hair. With her other hand she reached for a green rubber band and stuffed as much hair as she could through it.

She brought her face close to the mirror. Above one of her hazel eyes was a brow that could do with some plucking. Once upon a time she would have tended to that task immediately. Today it didn't seem to matter if she ever got around to it. She checked her other eyebrow, her nose and mouth. All of them looked fine, even to her own critical eye. Thanks to the months she had spent in the sun, her normally pale skin glowed. Phoebe wondered how anyone, herself especially, could look so wonderful on the outside and feel so rotten inside.

"Mirror, mirror, on the wall," Phoebe whispered. "Who's the fairest of them all?"

"*You* are, Phoebe," Phoebe imagined the mirror replying. "But you're not the richest. Tough luck, honey."

Phoebe winced. Was she losing her marbles? Wasn't losing all that money enough?

She remembered how her friend Kit Malloy had teased her for spending so much time with her face in the mirror. If anyone else had called her vain, Phoebe would have forgotten as soon as she heard it. But it hurt when Kit said it. Even the memory of the hurt hurt.

Kit and Phoebe. Phoebe and Kit. Until this summer Plymouth Island had meant the two of them together. Their friendship was practically an island tradition. When people saw Phoebe browsing in the shops along Commercial Street, they asked where Kit was. Very often this summer, Phoebe didn't know. This summer Kit and Phoebe had not started off well, and Phoebe had decided not to spend so much time with her. To keep from getting sad about that, too, Phoebe tried to be philosophical. Maybe it was a blessing that she and Kit weren't so close. Maybe it would make leaving Plymouth Island less unbearable.

Phoebe heard a rumbling in the hall. There were two sharp raps on the door before it flew open.

Violet O'Rourke, the Wilsons' maid, stood in the doorway. One hand was on her hip and the other was clasped to the handle of a steamer trunk that she had dragged down the hall. Violet was forty-three, which was old according to Phoebe. Violet wore no makeup and she never did anything about her hair, but Phoebe thought some people, like some things, should remain as they always were. As far as Phoebe was concerned, Violet O'Rourke should be forever.

"You still not up?" Violet asked, with a trademark gruffness that never fooled anyone

into believing she was anything but a senti-
mental marshmallow inside.

"Of course I'm up," Phoebe said.

"Up is dressed," Violet said, shaking her
head. "Up is orange juice and Rice Krispies
and bread that makes bodies grow in twelve
ways."

"Maybe later," Phoebe said, looking at
Violet and herself in the mirror.

"Maybe now," Violet chided. "So I can
get the packing done in peace and quiet."

"I promise I won't cry again," Phoebe
said.

"Honey, if you don't eat something, you
won't have the strength for another sob ses-
sion."

Phoebe turned from the reflection of Violet to Violet herself. "Are you making fun?"

"I've decided to hold you to your promise," Violet said, as she took Phoebe's favorite silk dress from a wooden hanger and began
to fold it. "You're going to tell your friends
the truth. Today, Phoebe."

Phoebe sat back in her chair and slowly
pushed the brush through her hair once more.
"I'm not up to it," she said. "I'm not feeling

very together today. It's still too soon." Although she wanted to feel better, she didn't believe that telling anyone about her family's problems would help. Just the thought of doing it made her feel sick. "Tomorrow I'll . . . think about it," she stammered.

She walked to the trunk and touched the dress. She remembered the day she had bought it. "I'll be outgrowing these clothes soon enough," she sighed. "The next clothes I get won't be any nicer than anyone else's. I won't be prettier than anyone else anymore. I wonder how many other twelve-year-olds have had to face the fact that the best part of their life is over?"

"That's all superficial stuff," Violet said.

"I happen to be *deeply* superficial," Phoebe admitted. "What of it?"

"Well, your family can't afford for you to be so superficial anymore," Violet said. "And you can't afford to be so secretive. It's turning you into a moper. Tell Kit."

"Tomorrow," Phoebe said. "Maybe."

"Don't you see what's happening to you, Phoebe?"

"Everything that could happen to me already has happened," Phoebe said.

"You'll end up a hermit. It's just a matter of time. Ducking your friends is just the first step."

"Are you going to be a pain about this?" Phoebe asked.

"Being a pain is one of the things I do best," Violet said. "It sure beats the heck out of cooking and cleaning."

"But what if Kit's not nice?" Phoebe asked. "She'll probably be smug and say it's about time I didn't get everything I want."

"You know Kit better than that."

"What if she's too nice? What if she feels sorry for me?"

"Do you think all you were ever good for was being rich?" Violet asked.

"Well, everyone did say I was awfully good at it," Phoebe said. "Do you know there are kids who admire how I shop? Not Kit and some of the others. They think I'm just rich and vain. Maybe they're right."

"Phoebe!"

"I guess I'm other things, too," Phoebe said uncertainly. "I'm bright, kind of, and I'm funny sometimes. I'm always sincere most of the time and I'm honest except when it comes to telling the truth. I mean, I don't lie too much, except about being poor now."

"And you're nice and you care about other people and you try to be helpful. And if you're not direct with the people who like you, they'll be disappointed. You know that, don't you?"

Violet tossed Phoebe a blouse and her favorite, most frayed cutoffs. Reluctantly, Phoebe got herself dressed. Violet loved her. Violet knew what was best for her. Violet wouldn't let her do something that wasn't in her best interest. It was too bad that Violet couldn't make her feel good about what she was supposed to do.

"Mirror, mirror, on the wall," Phoebe whispered. "Who's the most terrified of them all?"

Phoebe didn't wait for the mirror to speak. She already knew the answer.

2

THE WILSONS' HOUSE was as large as any on Plymouth Island and certainly the most elegant. The gray-brown shingles were replaced by the handyman whenever they looked the worse for wear, and the white trim was repainted every year. The gardener watered the lawns every day and the ten-foot-tall privet hedge along Dune Road was manicured once a month. Even the white gravel in the driveway was raked twice a week.

The place was too tidy, too peaceful. There was never anything to do unless you were a gardener or a maid. Once upon a time Phoebe had worried that her family had too much money. Now she felt sad that she didn't have to worry about anything so dumb ever again.

She took her bike from the garage and walked it to the end of the driveway. As beautiful as the gravel was, it was too thick to ride her bike on. When she got to the road, she sped toward town.

Closer to the village, the houses were smaller and closer together. They were also closer to the road. Phoebe saw kids playing in the front yards and had a momentary urge to slow down to peek through the windows. But today she sped on. If she didn't act quickly, she knew she might not act at all.

She turned onto Commercial Street. As it had been all summer, it was congested with cars and mopeds. Tourists clogged the sidewalks, examining the shop windows for the end-of-the-season sales.

On Water Street the traffic eased. Within a block or two there was only an occasional car or moped. Everyone who wasn't shopping today was out at the beach, getting the last of the summer sun.

Mrs. Edna Malloy's house at 37 Water Street was almost exactly like the Wilsons'.

The whaling captains who had built them long ago had been brothers and used the same plans. Both were enormous. Both were covered with the same gray-brown shingles, had the same white trim on the doors and windows, and porches that swept along the front.

But that was where the resemblance ended. There was nothing manicured about Mrs. Malloy's house. The house was well kept, but the unwatered lawn had turned brown during August. The picket fence could have used a fresh coat of white paint, and the cement walk from the street to the porch steps was cracked and rutted.

But the main difference was the barn. The Wilsons' barn had been replaced by a three-car garage and a gardener's shed. The barn at Edna Malloy's was still standing, but it wasn't a barn anymore. Long before Phoebe had been born, Mrs. Malloy had converted it into the Red Barn Theater. The last show of the season had closed last week. The actors and stagehands and apprentices had already left the island. It was another sign that summer was all but over.

Phoebe leaned her bike against the elm tree in the front yard and walked up the porch steps. As she knocked three times on the frame of the screen door, a wave of anxiousness swept through her.

"Kit?" she called, half hoping that Kit wasn't home. When she saw Kit skipping down the front stairs, she felt her heart skip a beat. Unless she were interrupted by an act of God, Phoebe would have to tell what happened.

"Hi there, Pheeb," Kit said as she stepped onto the porch and let the door slam behind her.

Over the summer Kit's light brown hair (which Phoebe had thought a little bit mousy) had bleached in the sun to a radiant blond, and her skin (which Phoebe thought a little sallow) had turned a deep tan. Phoebe wondered how anyone as pretty as Kit could be so indifferent to how she looked.

"What are you up to?" Kit asked as she sat down on the top step and gestured for Phoebe to join her.

"I was in the neighborhood," Phoebe said cautiously. "That's what I was up to."

"Which means you're on your way *to* somewhere," Kit speculated, "or you're on your way *from* somewhere. Do you want me to guess?"

"Guess what?" Phoebe asked.

"What you're doing in the neighborhood," Kit giggled.

"I'm seeing you is what I'm doing in the neighborhood," Phoebe said. "There's some stuff I wanted to talk over with you."

Kit turned to her. "You're mad at me again?" she asked.

"No, it's, well, something else."

"You're mad at Pink or Derek?"

"I'm not mad at anyone," Phoebe said, sitting up very straight. "It's about me. Maybe it's not such a good time to talk," she mumbled.

"It's as good a time as any," Kit said. "If you want to talk, I want to listen. That's what friends do, isn't it?"

Phoebe tried to speak. What she heard, however, was not the sound of her own voice, but the slam of the screen door. As she turned, she saw Kit's brother, Derek, standing behind her. Derek was thirteen, a year older than Kit and Phoebe. He had black hair and eyebrows that met above his nose. By anyone's standards, he was good-looking. By Phoebe's standards, he was the best-looking boy on Plymouth Island. At the beginning of the summer Phoebe had had the most severe but also the briefest crush on him. Although she didn't thrill when he was around, she couldn't help liking him still.

"The two people I most want to see!" Derek proclaimed in his most ingratiating, most insincere tone of voice. "One of my all-time favorite sisters with one of my all-time favorite friends of one of my all-time favorite sisters." Without waiting for an invitation, Derek plopped down between Kit and Phoebe and hugged each one. "Is this my lucky day or is this my lucky day?" he asked. "You tell me!"

"If you're looking for money, it is *not* your lucky day," Kit said sourly. "We're on to you, Derek, and so is everyone else on the island."

Derek withdrew his arm from Kit's shoulder and turned his now undivided attention to Phoebe. "You down on me, too, Phoebe?" he asked with mock fervor. "You got a kick out of meeting the ghost of Evangeline Coffin, didn't you?"

"Until I found out it was a scam," Phoebe admitted. "Imagine dressing up your other favorite sister in a sheet and getting everyone to pay to meet her. You should be thoroughly ashamed of yourself." Phoebe couldn't admit out loud that she had liked the caper even after she had found out it was a trick. For a whole week Evangeline Coffin had kept her from worrying about her own problems.

"And don't think for a moment that I'm not," Derek assured her, with a seriousness that struck her as surprisingly real. "I hadn't planned to feel bad about it for more than an hour or two, but it's two weeks and I'm feeling worse than ever. Grandma says I'd feel better if I made amends to the whole island. That's why I've got to talk to you."

"You gave back all the money," Phoebe said, relieved to be distracted again from her own problems. "Hasn't everyone forgiven you?"

Derek sat forward and rested his elbows on his knees. "The trouble is, I haven't forgiven myself," he said. "I have to *do* something more, something major."

"Are you trying to tell us that you really do have a conscience?" Kit said.

"If I had known, I wouldn't have pulled the Evangeline Coffin caper in the first place," Derek said forlornly. "Summer is over in a week, and if I don't make my amends to the island by then, I'm going to have one terrible fall, winter, and spring."

"How about a contribution to the fund they've set up to save the old Coffin mansion," Kit suggested. "It's where you staged the stunt. You owe the house something. And if they don't fix it up soon, it's going to fall down."

Derek put an index finger to his chin, signaling that heavy thinking was going on. "All I've got is five bucks. That wouldn't do anyone's conscience any good."

"Then raise some money," Kit said. "Turn yourself into a one-boy fund-raiser. Go door-to-door. I bet everyone would be happy to give something once they're assured it's not another scam."

"If you weren't my sister, I'd give you a great big kiss," Derek said, sounding as if he meant it, too. "Grandma's usually a soft touch. How about your dad, Phoebe? Is he feeling his usual generous self these days?"

"My father's still in Philadelphia,"

Phoebe said anxiously, remembering all at once why she had come to the Malloys.

"He'll be back, won't he?"

"Not for another week," Phoebe said. "Too late to help you, I'm afraid," she added, just in case Derek might think otherwise.

"Forgive my crudeness, but your father can make a difference to anyone's fund-raising activity," Derek said. "I'll call him in Philadelphia tonight!"

"You can't call him," Phoebe announced suddenly.

"Why on earth not?" Derek asked.

"My father is . . . is . . . is," Phoebe sputtered.

"Is there something wrong with your father?" Kit asked. "He's not sick, is he?"

"He's fine," Phoebe assured her. "Everyone's fine."

"Why wait till this evening?" Derek asked. "I'll call him now!"

The parts of Phoebe's body that were responsible for delivering the honest truth were paralyzed with fear. If Derek called, her father might tell him exactly what had happened. No matter what she had promised Violet, she knew she still wasn't ready for that. Phoebe racked her brain for something, anything, to keep Derek from putting through the call. "You'd be raising other people's money," she blurted out. "Wouldn't it be better for your conscience if you raised the money by earning it?"

From the way Derek stuck his index finger in his mouth, Phoebe could tell he was thinking hard. From the way he was biting down on his fingernail, she could tell he didn't like what he was thinking.

"You've got a point, Phoebe," he said sadly.

"I do?" Phoebe asked, amazed she had made sense.

"But how the heck am I supposed to make enough money to save the Coffin mansion? I'd better stick with other people's money. What is your father's telephone number?"

"We'll help!" Phoebe exclaimed. "Even if Kit and I aren't conscience-stricken, we're dying to do something for the Coffin mansion. Right, Kit?"

"Wrong, Pheeb," Kit said. "There's only one week of summer to go, and the last thing

I want to do is spend it making Derek's amends for him. I want to go sailing and water-skiing," Kit continued. "I want to have the best tan in my class back in Grandview Heights. What do I care about Derek's amends?"

"Don't you care about Plymouth Island?" Phoebe asked as dramatically as she could, even though she knew Kit loved Plymouth as much as she did.

"Other people love the island and they don't have to go around saving it," Kit said.

"Other people aren't as fortunate as we are," Phoebe replied.

"Are you shaming me into helping?" Kit asked.

"I'm appealing to your finer instincts," Phoebe said solemnly.

"You *are* shaming me into it!" Kit cried.

"I know you're too fine a person not to help," Phoebe said.

"You're not playing fair," Kit sighed. "Guilt runs deep in the Malloy family's veins."

"You won't regret it!" Phoebe said happily. Even though she felt a little guilty about pushing Kit's guilt button, she couldn't help feeling relieved, too. "Now all we need is a little plan."

Each one of them rested a chin on a hand and an elbow on a knee. After a minute they shifted to the other hand, elbow, and knee. Still no one said a word. Then Derek stood up and paced. Kit did the same. Then Phoebe joined them.

"I'm not getting anything," Phoebe said. "How about you guys?"

"Nothing," Kit said.

"My brain waves are dead," Derek said. "Maybe I'll just have to live with the guilt."

"Or go back to Plan A," Kit suggested.

"My father, you mean?" Phoebe asked.

"Not *just* your father," Kit said. "Grandma and Herb and the other grown-ups. Derek can go door-to-door, I'll go water-skiing, and Phoebe can go shopping."

"We can't give up," Phoebe said excitedly, pretending to ignore Kit's crack about shopping.

"What do we know about making an honest buck?" Derek asked. "It's lucky none of us has to earn our own keep. We'd starve to death."

"Speak for yourself," Phoebe protested.

"You're used to having more than we are," Kit reminded her. "You would starve to death *first,* Phoebe! When it comes to money, your only area of expertise lies in spending it."

"I know how to do other things with money besides spend it, Kit!"

"You make fun of how much you spend on clothes," Kit said. "Why can't I?"

"Because I am not just some helpless rich kid!" Phoebe said firmly. "For your information, Kit Malloy, not just any jerk can shop well."

"Any rich jerk can!" Kit laughed.

"So you think I'm a rich jerk, do you!"

"Calm down, Phoebe," Derek said, stepping between the girls. "We're not going to be able to come up with a money-making scheme on such short notice. I'll go back to Plan A. It'll be okay."

"It will not be okay," Phoebe insisted. "It'll be terrible! Give me one day, Derek, and I'll come up with a plan."

"All by yourself?"

"If it's the last thing I do on this island, I'm going to prove I'm not some silly twit who can always fall back on my father's money."

"Last thing?" Kit asked. "What are you saying? You don't have to prove anything to me. I'm your friend. Remember?"

Phoebe ran down the steps. As she grabbed her bike, she turned back to Kit and Derek. "I'll save the Coffin mansion single-handedly if I have to!"

Kit was running down the steps after her, but Phoebe was too angry to stay one more second. She jerked her bike onto the cement walk and jumped on. In no time flat she had taken the corner at the gate and was speeding down Water Street.

3

ON A NORMAL DAY Phoebe wouldn't have dreamed of interrupting Pink Cunningham while he was working. But today wasn't normal. It was turning into Phoebe Wilson's all-time worst crisis. As far as Phoebe was concerned, only Pink Cunningham could help her avert an all-out catastrophe.

All through the summer Cunningham's Boat Yard was as noisy as anyplace on Plymouth Island. But today it was so quiet that it was spooky. Phoebe wandered through the labyrinth of Boston whalers, catamarans, and skiffs waiting to be dry-docked for the winter. She looked through the window of Pink's father's office. No one was there. She was about to call out Pink's name when she saw the top of his head bobbing up and down on the other side of a sloop. As she stepped closer, she saw that Pink was painting the hull white.

"Pink?" she asked. "Are you the only one working?"

"There's not much to do around here now. "I'm just finishing this job before I start packing." He set his paintbrush on the lid of the can and turned to her.

"It's definite then?" she asked.

"Ten days from today I'll be at Winslow," he said.

"Excited?"

"I've never lived off the island before," he reminded her. "Before this summer I never even imagined going away to some boarding school."

Phoebe thought Pink was looking more than usually attractive this morning. His freckles had blended into a tan, thanks to working in the sun, and his hair was closer to strawberry-blond than pink. Even though he was anxious about Winslow, he looked so together that she momentarily forgot about her own feelings.

"Mackie Vanderbeck and I are going to be roommates," Pink continued. "We decided the other day, just before his family left the island. That'll make it easier, having Mackie around."

"Sounds like you're going to do great," Phoebe said. "I wish I could handle my affairs so well."

"What's wrong?"

"Poor Derek is conscience stricken about duping all the kids with his ghost scam," Phoebe explained, trying to stay composed. "He wants to make amends by earning money for the restoration of the Coffin mansion. But he doesn't have a clue as to how to earn the money."

Pink looked confused. "That's Derek's problem," he said.

"Well, since he can't come up with a way to make some money, I promised to do what I could. That's how it got to be my problem, too."

"Why get involved?" Pink asked. "Don't you have better things to do?"

"Is it wrong for me to want to help some worthy island cause?" she asked, knowing she was sounding a bit self-righteous but liking the sound all the same. "Do I have to apologize for wanting to do something nice?"

Pink smiled in a way that made Phoebe feel nervous about what he was thinking. "It's not wrong," he said. "It's just not right to get so upset about it."

"The truth is that Kit Malloy left me no other choice," Phoebe said, suddenly feeling all the more comfortable for having Kit to blame.

"What are you talking about?"

"She says I don't know anything about making money," Phoebe declared. She was stretching the truth and she knew it. But it was the only way she could make Pink help her. "She thinks I'm a bubble-gum head who would be totally helpless if my father weren't so rich." Phoebe stopped abruptly. Even if she hadn't meant to tell the truth, she hadn't intended to state an outright lie.

"She said you were a bubble-gum head?" Pink asked incredulously.

"Not in so many words," Phoebe hedged. "But I know that's what she thinks."

Pink reached for the thermos on the

ground. He poured lemonade into the cap and offered it to Phoebe. "When are you going to stop guessing at what Kit's thinking?"

"I know Kit," Phoebe insisted. "I know when she thinks I'm a loser."

"Aren't you kind of overreacting?"

Pink took a sip of the lemonade. He wouldn't accuse Phoebe of overreacting if he knew the truth, Phoebe thought. But as she realized she couldn't tell him the truth any more easily than she could tell Kit and Derek, the lemonade took a wrong turn between her mouth and her stomach and she began to cough violently. As Pink thumped on her back, she caught her breath and regained what equilibrium she was still capable of regaining.

"Tell me about your plan," Pink said.

Phoebe was glad she hadn't taken another sip. If she had, she would have been in the middle of another coughing jag. "The plan is what I came over to talk to you about," she said with forced cheeriness. "What do you think it ought to be?"

"You want me to come up with a plan?" Pink asked suspiciously.

Phoebe nodded as winningly as she could.

"You're so bright, Pink. Why, I think you're just about the brightest boy I ever met in my entire life."

"But, Phoebe . . ."

"As soon as I promised Kit and Derek a plan, I knew you were the perfect choice to come up with it," she said.

"Short of amputating your mouth, I don't know how to help you," Pink said.

"What about my mouth?" she asked. "You think I should have it . . . what?"

"You expect me to deliver on some promise you made?" Pink asked.

Phoebe drew back. "Are you mad at me?" she asked meekly. "I thought you would feel flattered."

"If I were you, I'd head right back to the Malloys and tell them that you were suffering from temporary insanity when you made the promise."

"I am not insane," Phoebe said testily.

"Would it be easier to tell them you were just being stupid?"

"You think I'm stupid?"

"Well, now and then. Now especially."

"I'll come up with something," Phoebe said. "No one has to worry about Phoebe Wilson. You be at the Malloys tomorrow morning. While I'm showing Kit and Derek that I can come through, I might as well show you."

"Are you mad at me now?" he asked.

"You're not making me feel good about myself, Pink," Phoebe said. "Don't you know how important self-esteem is to a person?"

"Your problem is you, Phoebe Wilson. Not me!"

Phoebe didn't understand what Pink was talking about now, but she wasn't about to ask him to explain. For the second time in one morning, Phoebe found herself pedaling furiously away from a friend. So what if everyone on Plymouth Island thought she was a jerk. It didn't mean anything, Phoebe told herself, except that everyone on Plymouth Island was wrong about her!

4

IT DIDN'T OCCUR TO PHOEBE until the next morning that everyone else might be right. A chill went through her body, and she wondered if she really was the biggest jerk of all time. As Phoebe got herself dressed and ready for breakfast, she tried to reassure herself that just because she sometimes acted like a jerk didn't necessarily mean she actually was one.

"I still think you should have," Violet said, as she poured herself a mug of coffee and settled herself across from Phoebe at the kitchen table.

"I couldn't," Phoebe insisted. "It was

the wrong time." She drained the last of her orange juice and took an extra-large spoonful of Rice Krispies. Rarely had she felt less hungry, but she hoped Violet would back off if she ate something. "I explained it all to you last night. Derek was too upset about his amends," she went on. "I've never seen him in such bad shape. And Kit was kind of a mess, too. What kind of friend would I have been to tell them something that was bound to upset them more?"

"And what was Pink so upset about that you couldn't tell him either?" Violet asked as she slowly stirred her coffee.

"He was packing for Winslow," Phoebe explained. "He hardly had time for more than hello and good-bye. He's *very* nervous about going away to school, Violet."

Violet shook her head and turned her gaze out the kitchen window to the gulls that were swooping over the bluff. "You're going to disappoint what friends you still have if you don't come clean. It will be hard enough to explain why you've waited so long to tell them your bad news. Sometimes friends can help, you know."

"But everyone will be too busy giving

me credit for saving the Coffin mansion," Phoebe said.

"You come up with a plan in your sleep?"

Phoebe bit her lip. "I'm working on it," she said. "Do I look worried?"

"It's hard to tell with you biting your lip so hard," Violet said. "You got into this fix just to keep Derek from finding out about your dad."

"There's no connection," Phoebe insisted. "If I had the time, I'd explain it to you." She looked at her watch. It was a quarter to nine.

When she pulled up in front of the Malloys' house, Derek was waiting for her at the picket fence.

"I sure hope you've got one great plan, Phoebe," he said. "I don't know how long I can take the pain."

"Pain?" Phoebe asked.

"It's my conscience," he moaned. "After all these years, I'm surprised it still has moving parts."

Before Phoebe could say anything, Derek was striding ahead of her. In the back she saw Kit and Pink sitting under a tree. As Phoebe caught sight of the sailboats and whalers and even a yacht bobbing gently in the harbor, she felt awful all over again that she wouldn't be back to see it next summer.

"You need a gavel to call the meeting to order?" Kit asked.

Phoebe sat on the edge of an aluminum chaise. Was Kit being mean or was she just making a joke, Phoebe wondered. Either way, Phoebe would have to ignore it if she were to finesse the ordeal that lay before her. "We need just ourselves, I think," she said evenly.

"Then all we need is the plan," Derek said cheerfully.

"I have devoted the last twenty-four hours to it," Phoebe announced. "The plan has been number one on my list of priorities, I can assure you."

There was an awkward silence before Derek spoke up again. "You did come up with a plan, didn't you, Phoebe?" he asked.

"I promised I would, didn't I?"

There was another, more awkward moment of silence.

"Would you like to share it with us?" Pink asked.

"Personally, I can't think of anything I would rather do this morning," Phoebe said.

"How about doing it now?" Kit suggested. "That's what we're here for, isn't it? Even one little plan is better than no plan at all."

"Maybe Phoebe came up with more than one plan," Pink said.

"That's it," Phoebe oozed. "There are just so many possibilities zooming around in my brain that I just can't decide where to start."

"Such as?" Derek asked. "Why not start with the A's?"

"Auctions," Phoebe stammered, nervous but grateful something, anything, had popped into her head. "What about auctions?"

"What do we have to auction off?" Kit asked.

"Which is exactly why *I* decided an auction wouldn't work," Phoebe said quickly. "That's why I thought of a . . . a . . . bazaar."

"Too much person power needed," Pink said. "And too much time needed to put one on. We have only a week."

"Just why I threw that idea away the very second I thought it up," Phoebe said agreeably, but she felt the chill inside her getting worse. She wished she had worn a down jacket and woolen mittens. Never could she remember a September morning this cold.

"And we can't get real jobs," Derek said. "So that's out. What did you finally decide we should do to benefit the restoration fund?"

"Benefit, benefit," Phoebe muttered. She had finessed and delayed as long as she could. She felt her chill turn into panic. "Benefit, benefit," she mumbled again.

"What a great suggestion," Pink exclaimed.

"She didn't make a suggestion," Derek said. "Not yet."

"She suggested a benefit," Pink said. "Say it louder so Kit and Derek can hear."

"Benefit," Phoebe said in a stronger voice. "We'll have a benefit!"

"Was that your idea all along, Phoebe?" Pink asked.

"Yes, it was, Pink," she lied happily. The chill was losing its bite and her blood was beginning to thaw nicely, too. "I am so pleased you like it."

"What kind of benefit were you thinking about?" Derek asked, suddenly looking more attentive.

"There are all sorts," Phoebe said, hoping one or two would come to mind and very quickly. "How about a raffle? My mother had one last year for stray animals."

"Raffles are boring," Kit said.

"How about a fashion show?" Phoebe asked.

"The Red Cross had one in July and the garden club had one in August," Derek said. "Who would pay to see another one?"

"I know," Phoebe said excitedly. "We could have a rock concert. On the stage of the Red Barn, too!"

"You got a group that would come?" Kit asked. "And play for free, too?"

Phoebe hoped she didn't look as helpless as she felt. "I was hoping you would have one, Kit."

Kit shook her head. "Scratch the rock concert," she said. "What's so great about Phoebe's benefit if we can't find a way to do it?"

Pink and Derek and Kit were staring at her, waiting for her to come up with her next suggestion. She thought of garden parties, house tours, and treasure hunts. All of them had been done and redone. How could she come up with something that had never been done before?

Suddenly Phoebe was startled by an enormous clang behind her. Everyone's eyes in the group, both of Phoebe's included, turned.

There stood Kit and Derek's eight-year-old sister, Margo. With her blond curls and crystal-blue eyes, Margo was as pretty as any eight-year-old should be permitted to get. In her hands Margo held cymbals that were almost as large as she was. She was wearing a bathing suit and a pair of high heels. On her head was a tiara.

"Where did you get that getup?" Kit asked.

"In the wardrobe room in the Red Barn," Margo announced as she clashed the cymbals together again. "Do I look gorgeous or just plain beautiful, or what?"

"You look weird," Derek said.

"I do not," Margo said vehemently. "I've never looked more ravishing."

"I say you look like Miss Weird of Plymouth Island," Derek insisted.

"Do not," Margo said. "I'm Miss Plym-

outh Island. Here I am," she continued, her voice becoming a tune. "I'm your dream come true."

Everyone was laughing and clapping now, but most especially Phoebe. As Margo continued to shout out her song, she took bow after bow to her audience. After every bow she crashed her cymbals harder. Deafening though the sound was, Phoebe was out of her mind with delight.

Now she knew exactly what the fundraiser would be!

5

"THE MISS PLYMOUTH island contest!" Phoebe shouted. "That's how we're going to save the Coffin mansion." She sat back in the chaise and stuck her pinky in one side of her mouth to keep her smile from getting out of hand. "It's perfect! Everybody loves beauty contests!"

"Sounds like a winner to me," Derek said. He was beaming, too. "You sure came up with a winner, Phoebe."

"With a little help from Margo," Kit said sourly. "You fudged your way through the whole thing. I bet you didn't have one single plan when you got here this morning."

"What's the dif?" Derek asked as he turned to Kit. "We needed one great plan and Phoebe's delivered it. There are five hundred seats in the Red Barn. At ten bucks a seat, that's five thousand dollars!"

"Wow!" Pink exclaimed. "It's enough to save the mansion!"

"You think big, Phoebe!" Derek added gleefully. "I like that."

Phoebe leaned forward and said, "Maybe Kit doesn't like it because I'm the one who came up with it. Perhaps Kit was under the mistaken impression that I am a hopeless twit."

Kit stood and began to pace around the circle of kids. "It's nothing personal, believe me," she said. "But a bunch of girls parading in bathing suits is pathetic. Who's going to buy tickets to that kind of spectacle?"

"It'll be fun, Kit," Phoebe said. "We'll wear our nicest bathing suits and we'll wear long dresses and heels and we'll get to say why we love living in America. We'll save the Coffin mansion and have a ball doing it!"

"You *want* to be in it?" Kit asked incredulously.

"Most girls would *love* to be in a beauty contest," Phoebe said, secure that being pretty was one thing she still did very well.

"What do I get to do in a beauty contest?" Pink asked.

"There will be plenty of work behind the scenes," Derek said. "Setting the stage, selling tickets. You can be part of that, Pink."

"But I'm never going to be Miss Plymouth Island," Pink said. "And I don't want to be behind the scenes."

"I want a beauty contest," Margo chanted. "I've always dreamed of being in one. Ever since I was a little girl. If I can't be in the Miss Plymouth Island beauty contest, I don't want to go on living."

"It's three to two then," Derek declared. "Pink and Kit are against it. Phoebe, Margo, and I are for it. Majority rules. Is that okay with everyone?"

"Not with me, it isn't," Pink said.

"Me either," Kit said. "Is Margo going to work on this contest?"

"Work? Me?" she asked suspiciously. "Except for winning it, I don't want to have anything to do with it."

"Then Margo's vote doesn't count," Kit said. "It looks like a tie to me."

"Looks like we need a judge," Phoebe said.

"How about *two* judges?" Kit asked. "Grandma and Herb are over at the theater."

A moment later the kids were marching toward the Red Barn. In one way or another, Mrs. Malloy and Herb had helped out every one of them and no one needed to take a vote about going to them with a problem.

The Red Barn Theater was separated from the Malloys' house by an asphalt parking lot. As Derek opened the lobby door, he yelled out, "Grandma! Herb!" One by one the kids peered through the box office window. The box office was empty. Derek opened the door to the auditorium and the rest of the kids followed him through it.

Phoebe had been to the Red Barn before, but only to see the plays. She had seen it when the dark red velvet curtain was down and the brass-plated houselights glowed warmly in their green shades along the sides of the auditorium. At night uniformed ushers handed out programs to theatergoers dressed in their best summer clothes. The Red Barn was festive, almost elegant, when a play was about to start.

The last play of the season had ended its run the previous Saturday, and the next season wouldn't begin until the following June. Now, for the first time, Phoebe noticed the unpainted cement floor that led down to the stage. She saw the tiny rays of sunlight poking through the holes in the walls. She noticed how worn the seats looked. But as Phoebe saw Herb holding out part of the curtain while Mrs. Malloy delicately, almost lovingly, patched it, she knew the theater was beautiful to them even under the glare of the naked bulb above the stage.

"You kids got a problem?" Herb Kramer asked, as he looked up at the small army approaching him. He was in his early sixties, Phoebe guessed, and he was trim and athletic, and his hair, though gray, was in a crew cut that made him look much younger.

"It looks like a posse." Mrs. Malloy laughed as she put aside her mending. She was wearing very red lipstick, a poncho, and black slacks. Even indoors she wore dark glasses, which Phoebe thought very sophisticated. Phoebe thought Mrs. Malloy and

Herb Kramer made a very sharp-looking couple, even if they were old enough to be her grandparents.

"We're not here to lynch anyone," Derek announced. "We want some advice."

"We want you to decide something," Kit corrected him.

"It's about me being Miss Plymouth Island," Margo added. "Phoebe and Derek say it's okay. But Kit and Pink are standing in my way."

"I'm just trying to make amends and my plan is to make a significant contribution to the restoration of the Coffin mansion," Derek said.

"And the rest of us want to help. I suggested that we stage a beauty contest," Phoebe added.

"They want to do it in the Red Barn," Kit said. "Do you want anyone to put on a sexist beauty contest in your theater, Grandma?"

"A beauty contest," Mrs. Malloy said, in a tone of voice that made Phoebe feel ill at ease right away.

"It's a little old-fashioned, isn't it?"

Herb asked, in a tone that suggested he didn't like the idea either.

"It's a sure money-maker," Derek said.

Mrs. Malloy took off her sunglasses and sat down on the edge of the stage. "Well, I'd be delighted to contribute the Red Barn for a night for a worthy cause," she said. "And the Coffin mansion is certainly worthy. I only wish the event were a little, shall we say, worthier."

"You don't like it?" Phoebe asked.

"I knew she wouldn't," Kit said. "The contest is off."

"But maybe something else is on," Mrs. Malloy said. "Couldn't we try to improve on the beauty pageant idea a bit?"

"Something we can all participate in," Pink said. "Behind the scenes and in front of the scenes, too."

Herb stepped forward. "How about a talent contest?" he suggested. "A young people's contest. I bet you kids could put on quite a show."

"You mean singing, dancing, that kind of stuff?" Kit asked.

"Anything your talented hearts desire,"

Mrs. Malloy said excitedly. "Oh, Herb, it's just the ticket."

Margo pulled at one leg of her grandmother's slacks. "It stinks," she moaned. "Who wants to pay to watch someone sing and dance when they could pay to see someone look pretty?"

"We can put up a sign-up sheet outside the lobby and spread the word," Pink said happily. "And I'll start rehearsing my vocal chords."

"How about doing some of your modern dance, Kit?" Herb asked.

"Maybe," Kit said, her face brightening at the suggestion. "I've spent enough time taking lessons back home."

"Can I be a drum majorette?" Margo asked uncertainly. "Do you think that counts as talent?"

"You better believe it," Mrs. Malloy said, as she hoisted Margo to the stage and let her march around as though she were already in the midst of her performance. "We'll need a master of ceremonies," she said. "Derek, do you think you could pull that off?"

"If you'll be our orchestra," Derek said.

"My piano and I are happy to volunteer," Mrs. Malloy said.

"I'll be stage manager," Herb said. "But we're going to need everyone working double time. Anyone think they can build a runway into the audience?"

"Easy," Pink said. "We can take all the scrap wood we need from the boat yard."

"I can help set up the lights," Kit volunteered, "when I'm not rehearsing my magnificent dance act, that is."

"And I'll do the publicity and start selling tickets," Derek said. "And the audience can be the judges. Whoever gets the most applause at the end wins Plymouth Island's first annual young people's talent contest."

"Think we can pull it off in a week?" Herb asked.

There was a loud cheer that rose instantaneously from everybody's throat.

Except Phoebe's. As *her* beauty contest had turned into *their* talent contest, she had (almost instinctively) stepped back from the group. As one kid after another got involved, she had taken a few more silent steps back up the aisle until she was halfway out of the auditorium. Not once had anyone asked her if she liked the idea of a talent contest, she thought resentfully.

"Phoebe, dear. You're not leaving us, are you?"

"I've got to, Mrs. Malloy. I'm due back home."

"But you can't leave without telling us what you'll be doing in the contest."

"I haven't decided," she said anxiously.

"But you'll be in it, won't you?" Herb asked.

"I hope so," she said in a thin voice.

"It's going to be lovely, just lovely," Mrs. Malloy said. "And it all started with you, Phoebe. We should all be very grateful to you for getting the ball rolling."

Phoebe couldn't say anything more. She gave a fainthearted wave and turned on her heels, so that she could get out of the Red Barn as fast as possible.

6

ND THIS ROOM, I believe, belongs to
the little girl," squealed the lady with the
high-pitched voice. "And this must be the little girl who belongs to the room!"

Phoebe let the movie magazine she was
reading fall to the floor as she jumped off her
bed and onto her feet. In the doorway stood a
woman she had never seen before, and behind
her stood a man and another woman she had
never seen before either.

"Well, *are* you?" asked the lady.

"I'm Phoebe Wilson," Phoebe said. Although the strangers were neither armed nor

dangerous, their arrival in her bedroom scared her.

"She *is* the little girl," the lady said gleefully to the man and woman. "I'm Fawn Pride from Buy with Pride Realty. And these lovely people are the Pearsons and they're here to look at your home. Mind if we peek around?"

Before Phoebe could answer, Fawn Pride was opening the door to Phoebe's closet. The other lady took a tape measure from her purse and began to apply it to the sides of the closet. The man stood by Phoebe's window, first examining the room, then the view of the lawns and the ocean beyond.

"You're going to buy it?" Phoebe asked the man.

"It's a beautiful house," he said noncommittally. "Hard to leave it, I bet."

"I haven't left it yet," Phoebe said abruptly. Scooping up the movie magazine, she rushed out the door and down the stairs.

Violet was standing in the front hall, holding the front door as two men hoisted Phoebe's steamer trunk onto their shoulders and angled it through the doorway.

"Say good-bye to your summer wardrobe," Violet said matter-of-factly. "But don't get too emotional. It'll be waiting for you in Philadelphia."

"I don't have any major emotions left in me today," Phoebe sighed. "I'm just plain old numb."

"A healthy twelve-year-old girl can't do better than numb?"

"It beats feeling sorry for myself, which is what I did when Daddy said we had to sell the house," she said. "It's better than being hurt by Kit or angry at Pink, which is what I did most of yesterday. I think numb's the best thing that's happened to me all week. I'm going to spend the rest of the summer watching game shows on TV. That should keep me numb."

"You're not going to spend even a little time on the talent contest?"

"I can't sing. I can't dance. I'd make a lousy drum majorette. When Mrs. Malloy asked me if I was going to be in it, I should have said no straightaway. When it comes to doing anything, I am a complete waste of time."

"You're in all those school plays back home," Violet said. "And you know as much

about getting yourself all dolled up as any respectable twelve-year-old girl should. You'll come up with something."

"After all I've been through this week, all I'm equipped for is being a human punching bag," Phoebe said, groaning a little. "Step right up and let Phoebe Wilson have it. And with everything else that's going on, how could I get up in front of all those people. If they don't think I'm a jerk, they'll feel sorry for me."

Violet put her arm around Phoebe's shoulder and pulled her close. "You've got a flair for the dramatic," she said. "The stage could be your calling, honey."

Phoebe pulled away. "What I have a flair for is not telling it like it is," she said. "I couldn't tell anyone about our not coming back next year even though you said I should. And when Derek wanted a plan, I promised to come up with one even though I couldn't do that either, not really."

"You can still tell them the truth," Violet suggested. "The whole truth about everything."

"I'll never be ready for that. I'll tell them I can't be in their contest."

"How are you going to explain that?"

"I'll come up with something," Phoebe said. "I always do, don't I?"

"Can't disagree with you there," Violet said.

Phoebe tried to ignore the disapproval in Violet's voice. Then she heard footsteps behind her. As she turned, she saw Fawn Pride coming down the stairs.

"They love it," she said excitedly, the pitch of her voice reaching new heights. "I just know they're going to take it. Two days on the market and we've got ourselves a sale! Isn't that wonderful?"

"Why, that's the nicest bit of news I've heard in a long time," Phoebe said as brightly and as phonily as she could. "In fact, it's just perfect."

On the last syllable of the last word, Phoebe's voice cracked and she could feel the tears welling up behind her eyes. She put her hands to her face and ran up the stairs.

Some days nothing worked.

Not even numb.

7

DURING THE NIGHT the wind shifted and the air grew colder. Clouds blanketed the sky, hiding the moon and the stars. By morning the first fall storm of the year was pummeling the island with the heaviest, harshest raindrops Phoebe could remember. As she snapped the window shade, she saw that the roses in her mother's garden were bending low, and some had even broken off under the assault.

Beyond the bluff the waves had turned gray and angry. White foam rocketed into the air and the beach had disappeared. Later, when the storm passed and the sea receded, the beach would be ankle-deep in seaweed and driftwood.

Phoebe wanted to pull down the shade and crawl back into bed. Perhaps Violet would bring her some hot chocolate and light the birch logs in the fireplace, even though they were meant for show. Today Phoebe wanted to pretend that life didn't exist beyond the walls of her bedroom.

Phoebe reached again for the tab but she didn't pull down the shade. Pretending would no longer make the world go away. Even so, she couldn't help hoping Violet would come to her rescue and save her from what she was about to do.

"Feel my forehead," Phoebe asked. "Is it a little feverish?"

"Cool as a cuke," Violet said.

"How about my glands? Swollen, aren't they?"

Violet felt under Phoebe's ears. "Honey, you've got perfect glands. Don't see any nasty red blotches on your face either. Sorry, Phoebe, but you're in excellent health."

Trying to take Violet's medical verdict in stride, Phoebe got dressed. The light blue parka, the one that made her hazel eyes look all the more hazel, was gone. Violet had sent it back to Philadelphia. Phoebe was reduced to wearing the ugly yellow slicker that didn't complement anything except her personality.

She rode through the wind- and rain-swept streets of Plymouth Island in record time. Protected though she was by the slicker, her face and her hair were soaking by the time she got to the theater. Outside, under the awning, was the contestants' sign-up sheet. Already half the page was filled with signatures. Derek had certainly spread the word.

Phoebe heard the sound of hammering coming from inside the auditorium. As she stepped through the lobby and into the theater, she saw Herb and Derek erecting the runway on the edge of the stage. Pink and Mrs. Malloy were standing in the far aisle, conferring under one of the exit lights.

Derek put down his hammer. "It looks like we've got the makings of a smash hit, Phoebe," he said.

"Already?" she asked.

"People were calling up for tickets before we got them printed," he said. "My amends are in the bag."

Phoebe looked up as Mrs. Malloy, a sheet of music tucked under one arm, led Pink to the center of the stage.

"Stand there." She gestured to a spot five or six feet from the edge. "You don't want to be on top of the audience. Really, Pink. I never knew you could write music. I can't say how impressed I am." She sat down at the upright piano at the back of the stage and put the music in front of her.

"You wrote this song?" Phoebe asked, as impressed as Mrs. Malloy was, but not as happily so.

"I wrote it in an hour and it sounds like it," Pink said. "If you don't like it, you don't have to tell me."

As Mrs. Malloy played a chord, Pink planted his feet firmly together. He took a deep breath. He closed his eyes and opened his mouth and sang out in a strong tenor voice.

Hail, Plymouth Island,
Star of the Atlantic Coast.
Your subjects salute you.
You're the island we like the most.

What if your skies are stormy?
What if your seas are rough?
You're the only island for me.
You're the island with all the right stuff.

From the keeper of the lighthouse
To the captain at his helm,
Every swab and lubber
Loves to dwell in your realm.

Pink closed his mouth. When he opened his eyes, Phoebe was certain that he had come to the end of his song. But it wasn't until she heard Derek and Herb and Mrs. Malloy applauding that she clapped, too. Phoebe heard more applause behind her. As she turned her head, she saw Kit walking down the center aisle with Margo tripping along behind her. Both of them were clapping for Pink, too.

"Does anyone think it's too corny?" Pink asked.

"If you're worried, you can always bring on an American flag at the end," Derek suggested.

"What's the flag got to do with it?" Margo asked.

"It's a guaranteed way to get the audience where you want them," Herb explained. "But Pink's song is nice and so is his voice. There's no need for desperate measures."

"Can I practice my number now?" Margo asked.

"I was here first," Kit said. "Grandma, will you play for me, too?"

She jumped onto the stage and handed her grandmother her own sheet music. As Mrs. Malloy played the first few bars, Kit struck a pose with both arms in the air. As Kit made her first movements, Phoebe stepped down the aisle to be closer to the stage.

For years she had heard about the modern dance lessons that Kit took twice a week back home, but she had never seen Kit dance. Now she saw a Kit she hadn't seen before, a Kit she hadn't known existed. Kit the athlete was instantaneously Kit the dancer, as she delicately pirouetted around the stage and then went into a series of comfortable twists and turns. As the music picked up tempo, Kit went into a succession of spins and leaps that almost made Phoebe gasp. Suddenly Phoebe was feeling an admiration for Kit that she hadn't felt for anyone she had ever met before, much less been best friends with.

When the others burst into loud, enthusiastic applause, she couldn't help feeling all the worse about herself. Phoebe forced a smile and stepped to the stage. "It's going to be a terrific show," she said, "but I can't be in it."

Mrs. Malloy rose from her piano stool and stepped downstage. "We're counting on all of you participating."

"Well, I can't," Phoebe said. "There's nothing wrong. I've just got reasons."

"Which you aren't telling us about," Kit said, looking stern as she wiped her face and shoulders with a towel.

"They're *personal* reasons," Phoebe announced. She turned and walked abruptly up the aisle and into the lobby.

Outside, the rain was pounding harder than ever, but Phoebe couldn't wait for it to stop. She had to make her escape now.

"Phoebe Wilson!"

"Kit?"

"How dare you not enter the contest!" Kit said breathlessly.

"Let's not make a big deal out of it," Phoebe said. "Please, Kit."

"But you can't quit and let the rest of us do all the work," Kit protested. "You owe us an explanation."

"It's something you wouldn't understand."

"Try me!"

"You don't know me at all, do you?" Phoebe shouted back. "There's no point in explaining *anything* to you." She felt her hands clench.

"Tell me," Kit said, grabbing Phoebe's arm. "Tell me what I don't know."

"What do you care?" Phoebe fought to free her arm from Kit's grasp. "Let me go. I'll scream if you don't," she said.

"Girls!"

Edna Malloy was striding toward them, with Margo at her heels. Margo looked excited by the fight. Mrs. Malloy looked worried and impatient.

"It's a knock-down-drag-out," Margo squealed delightedly.

"It's nothing, Grandma," Kit said, suddenly letting go of Phoebe.

"Phoebe?" Mrs. Malloy asked.

"It's nothing to get concerned about,

Mrs. Malloy," Phoebe said, trying to regain her composure.

"Those mean looks on your faces could scare a ghost," Mrs. Malloy said. "Are you two in the middle of one of your tiffs?"

"We've hardly begun," Kit said.

"It's the very end of it, Mrs. Malloy," Phoebe countered.

"May I suggest you both go directly to your tree house for a summit conference?" Mrs. Malloy asked.

"Can I go, too?" Margo asked, tugging at her grandmother's pants leg.

"It's between Kit and Phoebe," Mrs. Malloy explained.

"But they never let me go to the tree house with them," Margo cried.

"It's raining too hard," Phoebe said.

"It's too cold," Kit added.

"I don't mind the rain or the cold," Margo said blithely. "And there's no thunder or lightning."

"Some other time for you," Mrs. Malloy said as she put her hand on Margo's shoulder. "Right now I'm holding Kit and Phoebe to their pledge to meet at the tree house if they ever got into another of their feuds."

"We're not going to settle anything there," Kit said.

"There's nothing to settle," Phoebe added.

"Girls!" Mrs. Malloy said in her most commanding and most theatrical voice.

"Tree house," Kit sighed.

"Tree house," Phoebe echoed. Without bothering to wrap her slicker tight around her, she marched into the downpour.

8

PHOEBE PEDALED so hard that sweat began to pour down her forehead. It mingled with the rain and made her eyes sting. The slicker was smothering her and she threw back the hood. The rain couldn't make her hair any wetter than it already was. She swooshed through a puddle and the spray soaked her feet and legs. Her sneakers were heavy with water. If they weren't the last pair of expensive sneakers she might ever own in her life, she would have kicked them off.

She turned off Beach Road. After a few hundred yards the macadam ended and the road turned to dirt. After a few hundred yards more, the dirt turned to sand and Phoebe's bike came to a dead stop. She stood on the pedals and pushed hard, but the wheels were stuck in the sand.

The bike toppled over and she fell to the ground. She lay spread-eagle in the sand, the bike on top of her and the rain pelting her and her bike. "Darn Kit!" she yelled.

She kicked her bike off her. She stood and tried to wipe the sand off her clothes. She wiped the rain and sweat from her face and felt the sand in her hair. "Darn Kit! Darn Kit!" she screamed.

She considered backing out of the meeting at the tree house. She reconsidered. Exhausted and soaked, she didn't have the strength to make it home. The tree house was her only refuge, as if anyplace could be considered any kind of refuge. Phoebe staggered into the pine forest.

She and Kit had discovered the tree house all by themselves. It had been their sanctuary, their secret place, where they met daily the first summers they were friends. This year they had been there only after their fight at the yacht club in June.

They hadn't come to the tree house since,

but Phoebe still knew her way by heart. As she drew closer, she walked more slowly, more warily. Then she spotted the ladder leaning against the tree. Whenever they left the tree house, they left the ladder lying on the ground. Had they forgotten to do that the last time, or was Kit there already, waiting for her?

"Kit?" she called. "You up there?"

There was no answer.

Phoebe tilted her head upward and looked for a pair of blue-jeaned legs dangling from the tree house. "Kit?" she called again.

"I'm here, Phoebe."

"But I don't see you."

"Look behind you."

Phoebe turned. As Kit threw back her hood and unzipped the front of her parka, Phoebe could see that she was as dry as anyone could be during a Plymouth Island nor'easter. Phoebe looked at Kit's sneakers. They were practically dry, too. Somehow Kit had avoided all the puddles between the village and the pine forest. It made Phoebe feel all the more incompetent.

"Want to climb up to the tree house?" she asked.

"Probably drier down here," Kit said. She knelt and felt the pine needles on the ground. "They're not wet at all. Can you believe it?"

"I'll sit anywhere that isn't soaked," Phoebe said. She sagged against the trunk of the tree and let herself slide all the way to the ground. She took off her sneakers and socks. She leaned forward and took off her slicker and dropped it on the ground. She ran her fingers through her hair. It felt wetter and sandier than before. Phoebe suppressed a moan. It was possible that once in her lifetime she had felt worse, but she was sure that she had never looked worse. She knew, though, that Kit was so uninterested in people's looks that she wouldn't even notice.

"You're a mess," Kit said. "Were you in some kind of accident?"

"A lot you care," Phoebe said, not trying at all to hide her sarcasm.

"Well, I do," Kit said as she sat down beside Phoebe. "Just because I'm mad at you doesn't mean I want you to get hurt."

"I'm touched," Phoebe said. "I fell off my bike is all. And I got drenched in some

puddles. How did you manage to get here in one dry piece anyhow?"

"I know how to ride my bike *around* puddles. I'll give you a lesson sometime."

"You're being mean," Phoebe said.

"I feel mean, " Kit said. "Is it so hard to understand that?"

"Why should I care *how* you feel?" Phoebe asked. "You don't care how I feel."

"Tell me, then," Kit said softly. The gentleness in her tone caught Phoebe short. She was prepared for screaming and yelling and accusing, but not for Kit to sound as if she genuinely did want to understand. "What's going on, Phoebe? Is it something to do with why you came over the other day? You had something to tell me, only you never told me."

"I don't remember what I came over to see you about," Phoebe said sternly.

"Well, I wondered if there was a connection," Kit said. "I wasn't trying to pry."

"There isn't a connection, " Phoebe said more adamantly.

"If you can't remember, how can you be sure?" Kit asked.

"Drop it, will you?"

"Not till you tell me why you're not entering the talent contest."

"It's no big deal, okay?"

"You mean it's none of my business."

"You got it," Phoebe said. "Can I leave now?"

"Not till you explain."

"Look, Kit," Phoebe said. "There's nothing *to* explain. Believe me."

"You shamed me into helping to save the Coffin mansion," Kit accused her. "How the heck can you quit without any kind of explanation?"

"Well, I just did," Phoebe said.

"Rich kids don't have to explain."

"What did you say?" Phoebe asked, not believing Kit could be so cruel.

"I didn't say anything," Kit said.

"About rich kids?"

"You said that!"

"I did not!"

"I did!"

Phoebe saw that Kit's lips were as still as hers were. Both girls rose slowly to their feet. Kit looked to the east. Phoebe looked to the west. There was no one, no sign of movement.

"Up here!"

Phoebe looked to the sky, and half a dozen raindrops hit her in the eye. She hugged the tree and looked up once more.

There, with her head hanging over the edge of the tree house floor, was Margo. She was grinning.

"Margo Malloy!" Kit shouted. "You come down immediately!"

"Not till you cool down," Margo pleaded, the grin disappearing from her face.

"If you don't come down, I'll come and get you," Kit called. She grabbed for the ladder, but for once she wasn't quick enough. Margo was already hoisting it to the tree house.

"How the heck did you get here before we did?"

"I know a shortcut," Margo said, grinning now that she was safe again. "I've been here before. More than a couple of times. You two never use it. Why can't I?"

"Because it's not yours," Kit insisted. "And because it's rotten to snoop."

"Well, it's certainly not as interesting as I'd hoped," Margo admitted. "I thought the two of you would really go at it. You know what I mean?"

"You were rotten enough with that crack about rich people, Margo," Phoebe said. "If Kit doesn't get you when you come down, I sure as heck will."

"I didn't mean to criticize you personally," Margo said. "I mean personally I kind of envy you, Phoebe. With all your money, it doesn't matter what anyone thinks of you."

"But I'm not . . . not . . ." Phoebe stammered.

"Not rich?" Kit laughed.

"What does rich ever have to do with anything?" Phoebe asked, not at all sure she wanted any kind of answer. "I wouldn't be in the contest if I were poor."

"Maybe," Kit sighed. "But still you ought to explain."

"Which she is not about to do," Margo chirped from on high. "Because she's rich and doesn't have to."

"Because," Phoebe muttered. "Because. Because I've decided to be in the show after all." It was the second to last thing in the world she wanted to do, but it kept her from telling the truth about everything, which was the very last thing she could ever do now.

"You mean it?" Kit asked excitedly.

"I mean it," Phoebe said solemnly, hoping that she wasn't about to see her whole life flash before her as people did just as they were about to die.

With every lie, every half-truth, every evasion, she had dug herself deeper into the worst hole of her entire career as a human being. In a few days she would pay for all her sins by making a complete and total fool of herself in front of everyone on Plymouth Island.

Kit reached out her arms but Phoebe drew back a bit. "I guess there really wasn't a reason," Kit said. "It was just a . . ."

"Silly rich girl's momentary whim," Phoebe said.

"Well, maybe you're a *little* silly, Phoebe, but if you had a real explanation, you would have told me."

"You bet," Phoebe added. One more lie couldn't make things any worse than they already were.

"I'll come down now if no one's mad at me," Margo said. Inch by inch she lowered the ladder to the ground. As she tentatively put one foot onto the top rung, she asked, *"Is anybody mad at me?"*

"No one is going to kill you," Kit admitted.

"Or even maim you even if you deserve it," Phoebe added.

Suddenly the rung broke and Margo lost her grip. Her slide turned into a fall, and in a split second Margo was sprawled on the ground. Her body was as still as it was silent. Immediately Phoebe and Kit knelt on either side of her.

"Margo, are you . . . ?" Kit asked anxiously.

"Well, I'm not dead, if that's what you mean!" Margo bawled as she sat upright. "But I might as well be! My arm! It's broken, I think."

"Thank heaven it's only your arm," Phoebe said.

"Easy for you to say!" Margo cried. "What's a drum majorette with a broken arm? It's an ex-drum majorette! How am I going to be in the contest if I have a broken arm?"

A few minutes later Kit and Phoebe had

balanced Margo on the handlebars of Kit's bike, and Kit was riding Margo to the emergency room of the Plymouth Island Hospital. Phoebe followed. If only she had been smart enough to break her arm and get out of the contest, she thought. Some people, she decided, had all the luck!

9

WHEN PHOEBE GOT BACK to the
Red Barn, she was exhausted. With her next
to last ounce of strength she added her name
to the sign-up sheet. How had she landed herself in this jam, she wondered. How on earth
had she let Kit manipulate her into doing exactly what she had been most desperate to
avoid?

As she rode home on her bike, Dune Road
turned into the talent contest. On one side of
the white line stood Phoebe mute and motion-
less on the stage of the Red Barn. On the
other side was an angry mob of an audience,
jeering, booing, and throwing rotten eggs at

the formerly little rich girl now turned poor. With her very last ounce of strength, she pedaled her weary self the rest of the way home.

Violet was scrubbing the kitchen floor. "Take off all your wet clothes on the porch before you set one foot inside this house," she warned.

"What if someone sees?"

"No one's around to see."

"It's not very dignified," Phoebe said.

"It's not very dignified for me to mop floors every hour on the hour," Violet said.

As the last piece of wet and sandy clothing dropped to the porch floor, Violet finished scrubbing and handed Phoebe a terry-cloth towel that was so large Phoebe could wrap it around herself two and a half times.

"What were you doing out in the rain?" Violet asked.

"Taking care of some personal business," Phoebe said. "I'm not at liberty to discuss it with you at the moment."

Violet shrugged and began to peel onions at the kitchen counter. "You're entitled to your privacy, honey," she said. "But if you ever need bail money, give me a call. Otherwise, I won't pry."

"Thank you for respecting my privacy," Phoebe said, drying herself.

Violet picked up a knife and cut the onions into quarters. She dropped them, quarter by quarter, into the food processor.

Phoebe started toward the hall. "You said I probably do have some performing skills," she said, as she suddenly turned on her heels. "Could you maybe name one?"

"You decide to be in the contest after all?"

"Kit and I had a little talk," Phoebe said slowly. "I decided I would be ignoring my civic duty if I weren't in the contest."

"What's Kit doing?"

"Some stupid dance thing," Phoebe said.

"Then why don't you do some stupid dance thing, too?"

"She's taken lessons," Phoebe said.

"Then do something else."

"But what?" Phoebe asked.

"Take a shower, Phoebe."

"Onstage?" Phoebe asked. "In front of all those people?"

"How about right here?" Violet asked. "How about right now? How about letting me get dinner started?"

"You don't care, do you?"

"I'm trying not to pry," Violet said.

Phoebe pulled the towel tighter and stalked off to her bathroom. She adjusted the water in her shower until it was the perfect hot-but-not-too-hot temperature. She touched her hair. There was more sand in it than on all the beaches of Plymouth Island. It would take hours, possibly days, for the water to rinse all the sand away.

"Hail, Plymouth Island," she said quietly, so quietly that she could barely hear herself above the roar of the shower. "Star of the Atlantic Coast. Your subjects salute you. You're the island we like the most."

Phoebe was amazed that she remembered the first stanza of Pink's song even though she had heard the words only once. As she started the second verse, she raised her voice slightly. "What if your skies are stormy? What if your seas are rough?" she sang louder and louder, surprised still by her recall.

But there was still more sand in her hair. Phoebe adjusted the water so that the stream from the nozzle turned into a jet spray. She sang, "Hail, Plymouth Island" again. When she reached the last lines, she was still feeling surprised, but not by her memory. It was her voice that was thrilling her now.

She remembered third grade in Philadelphia when the class had risen to sing "My country 'tis of thee. . . ." She had sung it as loudly as she could, and by the end of the song there wasn't one student in the classroom who wasn't looking at her peculiarly.

Was she sharp? Had she been flat? Mrs. Perkins, the teacher, had suggested Phoebe sing a little less loudly so that her voice could "blend in" with the other children's. Mrs. Perkins said her voice was "different." From that day on Phoebe mouthed the words the other kids were singing.

But the sounds that were coming from her throat now were sweet and mellow. She could sing! She could sing! Something had happened to her vocal chords over the years. They had matured just as Phoebe had, and her voice had blossomed along with the rest of her.

She turned off the water and stepped out of the shower. She wrapped another towel around her, looked in the mirror, and began to comb her hair.

Even by her severest standards, Phoebe looked wonderful once more. When her hair dried, she would look even better. Out the window she could see that the sun was shining. The storm had passed. She would skip the hair dryer and let the sun do the job.

As quickly as she could, she got dressed, grabbed her hairbrush, and ran down the stairs. Violet was standing by the kitchen sink with her hands on her hips. In the sink, pots and pans were piled high.

"What's going on?" Phoebe asked.

"There's no hot water," Violet said. "Our little songbird used it all in her shower."

"You heard me?" Phoebe asked happily.

"Couldn't help hearing you," Violet said.

"All along I thought I couldn't sing. Now that I can, I have something to do in the contest. Isn't that great?"

"I'm happy for you, honey. When there's some more hot water, I'll be happy for me, too."

"I have a really lovely singing voice, Violet. It's a gift, and I couldn't have received it at a better time. Did you like it, too?"

"From the shower it sounded like noise to me."

"I'll sing for you now," Phoebe said. "Outside, while my hair dries."

"Sing for Pink, too," Violet said. "He's working on the storm windows." She led Phoebe onto the back porch. Pink was taking down a screen and setting a storm window in the frame. All summer he had worked one or two afternoons a week at the Wilsons'. Phoebe realized it was the last time he might come, and she pushed the dreary thought from her head immediately.

"I'm in the contest after all," Phoebe said to him. "Did you know that?"

"I saw the sign-up sheet," Pink said. "I'm glad you had a change of heart."

"I've been practicing with your song," Phoebe said. "But I'll get another one for the big night. Would you like to hear me sing your song anyway?"

"I'm all ears," Pink said, leaning another screen against the side of the house and sitting down on a wooden bench.

Phoebe folded her hands in front of her and took a deep breath. She smiled for Pink and Violet just as she would for the audience at the Red Barn and took another deep breath.

The first notes sounded odd. Phoebe stopped and took another breath. She began the song once again. "Hail, Plymouth Island," she bellowed. It sounded even odder this time, not unlike her rendition of "My country 'tis of thee" in third grade.

Who was she kidding? Her voice was horrible! If anything, it had deteriorated with time. She looked helplessly at Pink and Violet. Violet's jaw was clenched and Pink was staring into space. Phoebe got to the end of the second verse and stopped. She wanted to cry. "Is it as bad as I think?" she asked. "Tell me I'm my own worst critic. Please, Violet. Pink, tell me it's okay. Tell me even if it isn't true."

"It's sort of an interesting voice," Violet said. "It's unusual. Personally I'm very fond of unusual voices. And, you know, voices don't always sound the same out of the shower."

"I hate it when you try to be nice, Violet," Phoebe wailed. "Don't be nice, Pink. Be honest."

"It's the song," Pink said. "It's a dumb song. No one could make it pretty."

"You're both being kind," Phoebe cried. "I thought you were my friends. How could I be so dumb as to think I could do *anything* right?"

"Get ahold of yourself, Phoebe," Pink said consolingly. "It's a talent contest. It's not the end of the world."

"It's the next worst thing!" Phoebe cried.

"You're talking crazy," Pink said. "Your singing isn't that bad."

Phoebe felt her face grow hot and her hands begin to tremble. Suddenly she was losing control of everything she had been hiding inside. "My father's lost a lot of money," she said. "We had to sell the house. Ask Violet if you don't believe me. I'm never coming back to Plymouth Island."

Pink turned to Violet. "It's true?"

Violet nodded sadly. "She wanted to tell you earlier but . . ."

"But I couldn't," Phoebe sobbed. "I couldn't tell you or Derek, and especially I couldn't tell Kit. It was like lying, but I was afraid to tell the truth. I didn't know how you'd react, whether you'd make fun of me for not being able to afford what I've always had or feel sorry for me. I started making crazy promises that I couldn't keep and it's just been getting worse. Now it looks like I'm going to stand on the stage of the Red Barn Theater and prove once and for all that I'm one of life's big losers."

Phoebe heard a cough behind her. As soon as she turned, she wished she hadn't. Kit was standing on the lawn. She looked stricken.

"You were afraid to tell me?" Kit asked.

"Of what you'd think," Phoebe moaned. "I'm so sorry, Kit. I've never been sorrier about anything in my whole entire life."

"And promising to come up with a plan for Derek's amends," Kit said. "Was that one of your crazy promises?"

"If Derek called Daddy, Daddy might have told him about what happened," Phoebe said. "I couldn't handle it, Kit."

"You didn't care about the amends or the Coffin mansion or any of it," Kit said.

"I *do* care," Phoebe protested. "I love Plymouth Island. But it's not why I got involved," she confessed.

"And got the rest of us involved, too," Kit said. She laughed but not happily. Her laughter was cold. "I come over here to apologize for bullying you about the contest and it turns out the contest is just your way of keeping something from your friends, something we might have helped you with. Do you know how that makes me feel, Phoebe?"

Phoebe didn't have time to answer. Before she knew it, Kit was tearing across the lawn. Phoebe started after her but her knees were shaking too hard. As Kit rode away on her bike, Phoebe collapsed onto the bench.

"Do you hate me, too, Pink?" she asked.

Pink shook his head. "You were upset and confused," he said. "I can understand that. Kit will come around. You'll see."

"She hates me," Phoebe said, knowing that as long as she lived, she would never forget the disappointment she had seen in Kit's eyes and heard in Kit's voice. "You're wrong, Pink. She's going to hate me *forever.*"

All along she had been upset, but never had she imagined being as upset as she was now. As far as Phoebe was concerned, the last piece of her world had finally come crashing down on her.

10

THAT NIGHT she called Kit three times. The next morning she tried again. Each time Kit refused to speak to her. What was the point in trying to apologize anymore? What was the point in hoping Kit would ever understand?

"It's what I deserved all along," Phoebe said bitterly.

"What's that, honey?"

"To be loathed and despised," Phoebe said. "What else?" She spotted another shell in the seaweed and dropped it in her pocket. The storm had left behind drier weather, which seemed to want to stick around for a while. It was too beautiful to stay away from the beach. Besides, with Pink finished for the summer, except for the windows, and with the two gardeners and the handyman let go, there was no one left except Phoebe and Violet to rake the seaweed from the beach.

"Why do you deserve it?"

"All my life I've been so high and mighty, only I didn't know it," Phoebe said. "I bet there are a lot of people who resented me for having everything I wanted. It's only right that I should grovel now. Yesterday with Kit was just a rehearsal for the talent show. That'll be my final humiliation."

"You're staying in it?" Violet asked.

"I deserve to be punished!" Phoebe announced stoically.

"Gee," Violet said. "You could be a regular role model for a whole generation of twelve-year-olds who have hit the skids."

"It's not as though I've lost everything," Phoebe said bravely. "I've still got my pride."

"Remember that when you're on the stage of the Red Barn," Violet said.

"It's a promise I'll keep," Phoebe said. "No matter what they throw at me."

"Decided what you're going to do yet?"

"Well, I won't sing," Phoebe said. "I'm not that sadistic!"

As they stood with the waves splashing around their ankles, Phoebe heard someone shout her name. She saw Derek and Margo standing at the top of the bluff. As they started down the stairs, Derek waved. Margo didn't because she couldn't. One of her arms was wrapped around a picnic basket. The other arm was in a sling.

"We heard, Phoebe," Derek said, as soon as he hit the bottom step, "and there's no reason to be embarrassed. Not with us."

"Kit told you?"

"We got the gist from her," Margo said cheerfully, "but we didn't get any of the gory details."

Violet laughed. "I heard *your* gory details, Margo. How's the arm?"

"It doesn't hurt at all," Margo said. "But keep it under your cap. If people find out I'm not in a lot of pain, I'm going to lose out on a lot of sympathy."

"Your secret's safe with me. How you taking missing the contest?"

"Very heroically, thank you, Violet," Margo said. "To prove it, I even brought Phoebe a little something in her time of need." She held out the basket.

"A picnic?" Phoebe asked, as Violet waved good-bye and started to walk up the hill.

"It's no picnic, believe me," Margo observed. "Look under the cloth."

Phoebe lifted the blue-checked cloth slowly and peeked. What she saw was not anyone's idea of a picnic. She didn't know if she should be appalled or only slightly bewildered.

"It may not be what you've always wanted," Margo said. "But it's what you'll need where you're going, wherever that is."

"Shoes?" Phoebe asked, as she raised the left half of a very tired, very elderly pair of loafers.

"I found them in the wardrobe room backstage," Margo explained. "They've seen better days, but they should get you through your first winter. And the can of spinach I took from Grandma's kitchen. She'll never notice it's missing, so there's no reason to feel guilty about my stealing it for you. And I bought the can opener with my own money. That's so you can open the can anyplace. Under bridges. In alleys. While you're hopping freight trains."

"You think I'm going to need all this stuff?" Phoebe asked, amused at Margo's misunderstanding.

"We're your friends," Margo said. "You don't have to pretend anymore. Not with us."

Phoebe began to laugh. At Margo, who without knowing it was absolutely right. But Phoebe laughed at herself mostly. At the way she had been carrying on.

"She's lost her mind, Derek," Margo said anxiously. "It has all been too much for her. You know how thin-blooded these rich kids are."

Phoebe laughed louder than ever now. "It's perfect. It *is* what I needed. Exactly."

"I told you," Margo said to Derek.

"Not the basket," Phoebe said. "I needed you. You and Derek. Just as you are. Right now."

"You may not like to think you need this stuff, but . . ."

"Margo, we've lost the house," Phoebe explained. "But we haven't lost anything else. My father still has his business in Philadelphia and we still have our house there. I'm going to the same private school I always went to. Violet's going to stay, too."

"Are you trying to tell me you're not a pauper?" Margo asked.

"Exactly," Phoebe assured her.

"Then give me back my basket," Margo said indignantly. "If you're not going to be destitute, I'm not going to feel sorry for you."

"You're not mad at me for not being totally down and out, are you?"

"I'll get over it," Margo said. "It's not your fault you're not lying in the gutter."

"Is Kit still mad at me?" Phoebe asked Derek.

"I don't know," Derek said. "When she got home yesterday, she told us what had happened to your family. We wanted to talk to her, but she wasn't in any mood to talk to us. This morning she barricaded herself in her room."

"Practicing her dance routine?" Phoebe asked.

"Oh, she's not doing that," Margo said. "She said she's going to work up something totally new."

"And she won't tell anyone what it is," Derek added. "No one's going to find out till the night of the contest."

"But that dance routine is fantastic," Phoebe said. "How could anyone, even Kit, come up with something better?"

"What's it matter now?" Margo asked. "You've got the contest in the bag. Everyone's saying you're going to win, Phoebe. The rest of us don't stand a chance against you."

"Me?" Phoebe asked, totally amazed. "People think I'm going to win?"

"You're very popular around here," Derek said pleasantly.

"Basically everyone feels very sorry for you," Margo said not as pleasantly. "You got the sympathy vote nailed down."

Phoebe didn't want to believe it, but she had to admit to herself that Margo was making a kind of perfect sense. If someone else were in Phoebe's shoes, Phoebe knew she would vote for them for all the wrong reasons, too.

"I am *not* pathetic," Phoebe announced.

"I'm going to prove it, too. I'm going to prove it *at* the contest." Suddenly Phoebe knew exactly what she was going to do, and she was going to do it so perfectly that she would end up a winner—even if she lost.

11

YOU'RE ALL LOOKING mighty talented tonight," Herb said jovially. "Each and every one of you." He smiled reassuringly at the kids standing in line offstage. He signaled for Mrs. Malloy, who was sitting at the piano on the other side of the stage. After she had played a few rousing chords, Herb began to pull the heavy ropes that made the curtains glide apart.

Phoebe heard the rustle of programs and chatter subside in the audience. She peeked around the proscenium. The theater was packed, with folks even sitting in folding chairs in the center aisle. She felt the sweat on her palms. Even though the other kids looked nervous, Phoebe knew in her heart of hearts that not one of them, not even Kit, could feel as nervous as she did. All they had to worry about was whether they would win or lose. Phoebe had much more at stake.

"Welcome, welcome!" Derek bellowed as he took center stage. He was wearing a blue seersucker suit, a pink shirt, and a very loud yellow tie. His outfit looked more like a costume than real clothes, Phoebe decided. "Tonight is the first annual talent contest for the benefit of the restoration of the old Coffin mansion. Thanks to your generosity, we gave the restoration committee a check for five thousand dollars this afternoon!"

There was a great round of applause and cheering from the audience. Phoebe felt the other contestants shifting nervously around her. The boy next to her was looking almost green. On the other side of him stood Kit, wearing a lavender evening dress, and looking over and over at a piece of wrinkled paper that she held in both hands.

Phoebe had nodded to her when she had arrived at the theater. Kit had nodded back and looked as though she were about to say something. Phoebe had felt herself tense up. Kit had seemed to sense it and stepped away. Phoebe wasn't about to deal with anything Kit felt like slinging at her tonight.

Since the morning with Derek and Margo, Phoebe had devoted all her time and energy to putting together her act for the show. She had retired to her bedroom and come out only for meals. She had spent hour after hour rehearsing in front of her mirror. From now on Phoebe was going to avoid mirrors. Briefly she had wondered, though, if maybe Kit had a point when she had called Phoebe vain. It didn't matter. Her days in front of the mirror were in the past.

"Our first contestant is our youngest," Derek announced from the center of the stage, with a heartiness that was kind of winning even if it didn't sound very sincere. "A future Dallas Cowgirl if there ever was one. Ladies and gentlemen, give a big Plymouth Island welcome to—" Derek turned to the wings. "What did you say your name was?"

"Margo Malloy, you creep," Margo whispered from the other side of the stage.

"Margo Malloy!" Derek shouted.

"Margo?" Phoebe gasped.

"She decided at the last moment," Pink explained.

"But her arm . . ."

"She said if you were going to corner the sympathy market, she was going to give you a run for it."

Phoebe watched Margo march onstage. Her drum majorette outfit was all red and blue sparkles. She wore little pink boots, and her baton had pink cotton puffs at either end. The best part of her costume was the sling for her arm. It was covered in pink sequins.

Phoebe watched her stride onstage and bow deeply to the audience. "Woweeee!" she screamed delightedly. She threw her baton in the air. As she reached for it, it fell to the ground. Margo seemed to be the only one in the theater who was in any way surprised by her miss. She winced as the baton rolled into the audience.

A man in the front row handed it back to her, and she threw it into the air again. Not so far this time, but she missed anyway. She picked up the baton again and clutched it to her chest. She ran offstage and returned a moment later, waving an American flag in one hand and her baton in the other until her music came to an end.

Then it was Pink's turn. His voice cracked on the first line, but as soon as the audience realized his song was an ode to their island, they roared their approval. By the time the song was through and Pink was taking his bow, he had made a big hit.

Another boy was next. Phoebe didn't know his name, but she decided right away that she didn't like him. Whatever-his-name-was was too calm and too self-assured for any other kid to like. He sat down at Mrs. Malloy's piano and skipped through the Minute Waltz in forty-six seconds.

Another boy, a juggler, followed the pianist, and then came a girl who played the guitar and sang a song against insecticides. Phoebe tried to keep paying attention to the other contestants, but she was too nervous about her own performance. What if everyone laughed at her? What if nobody laughed?

A girl who did gymnastics was tumbling and somersaulting on a mattress she had brought to the theater. At the end she walked off the stage on her hands and then sprang up to her feet to take her bows.

"And now," Derek called out as he took center stage again, "Miss Phoebe Wilson. Phoebe hasn't given us a clue as to what she'll be doing this evening, but if Phoebe's going to do it, it's going to be a treat."

Phoebe staggered onstage. Very slowly she turned to the audience. She smiled, but her heart wasn't in it. All she wanted to do was run. She looked to the third row. There was Violet. Maybe if she pretended Violet was the only one in the audience, she could get through it.

She tried to open her mouth but her lips were stuck. Her mouth was as dry as parchment and her hands were sweatier than ever. If she tried hard enough, sounds, maybe even words, would come.

"Hi, I'm Phoebe," she said, so softly that even she could barely make out what she had said. "I'm Phoebe Wilson."

"Hi, Phoebe!" people in the audience shouted back at her.

Phoebe hadn't been prepared for that, and she jumped back a little. But it was a friendly response, and for the first time Phoebe felt an iota of hope. "A funny thing happened on the way to the contest tonight," she said a little more loudly. "I met a man who was leaving his wife because her coffee was so bad. You want to know how bad her coffee was, folks?"

"How bad was it, Phoebe?" the audience asked in unison.

"Her coffee was so bad the judge said it was grounds for divorce," Phoebe said.

The audience laughed. Even though that was what Phoebe had prayed for, the laughter startled her. As they continued to laugh, however, she started to feel calmer. She took another deep breath and walked closer to the edge of the stage.

"Does anyone here know how to get down off an elephant?" Phoebe asked. She heard the quiver in her voice and hoped the audience didn't.

"How do you?" the audience hollered.

"You don't get down off an elephant," she said. "You get down off a duck!"

The audience groaned. They laughed and there was a smattering of applause. Phoebe felt her confidence grow. When she opened her mouth to speak, she could barely detect the quiver that had been there before.

"My father was so mad last week," she

said. "He said his shaving brush was ruined. I told him it looked okay when I used it to paint my dresser."

She heard the laughter and the applause at the same time now. She dared to look straight out into the audience. The people looked happy and friendly.

"Anyway, my father says kids are spoiled today," she continued. "He says when he was a boy he thought nothing of walking five miles to school. I told him I didn't think so much of it myself."

There was more laughter, more applause. Phoebe stepped closer to the audience. Why should she be afraid anymore? They liked her.

"Did you hear about the man who tried to rob the Plymouth National Bank the other day?" Phoebe asked. "He told the teller to give him all the money or else. The teller said, 'Or else *what?*' and the crook said, 'Don't get me confused. It's my first job.' "

The groan was louder than the applause, but it was a friendly groan. She decided they were ready for one more.

"I was starving last week for some seafood, so I went into the Sea Shanty Restaurant and asked the waitress if they served crabs, and the waitress said to me, 'Oh, we serve anyone.' "

Phoebe looked to the wings. The other contestants were laughing now, all except Kit, who was still studying that old piece of paper. Kit didn't seem to care anymore. But Phoebe was determined that she wouldn't let that bother her. She took her bows to the audience and ran off the stage.

It was a miracle. It was a triumph, her own personal triumph. No one, but no one, would vote for her because they felt sorry. If Kit was the only holdout to her performance, so be it.

Herb kissed her as she came off the stage. "I had no idea you were a stand-up comic," he exclaimed. "Did you, Kit?"

"You were good," Kit said.

Phoebe couldn't hide her skepticism. If Kit had come up with an act that was even better than her dance routine, she could afford to be generous, even to an ex-friend.

Derek announced Kit's name and Phoebe noticed how nervous Kit seemed as she walked on the stage. Her face had the mobility of a piece of granite, but her hands were clearly trembling when she held out the piece of

paper in front of her. "It's a poem," Kit said, her voice shaking a little.

"Louder! Can't hear you!" called a voice at the back of the auditorium.

"It's a poem," Kit said louder, but still uncertainly. "It's by me."

I looked in you and saw myself.
What you were feeling, I felt, too.
I made fun when you looked in the mirror.
But you were my mirror, my friend.
When I was filled with joy and hope,
It was the same for you.
When I was hurt and angry,
My mirror showed that, too.

Phoebe stepped closer to the stage. Kit's poem was about her, about them!

But sometimes I'm not clear to me.
My mirror lets me down.
Was that doubt yours? Was that fear
mine?
Was it the other way around?
Your feelings aren't the same as mine.
The reflection's just pretend.

112

When my mirror failed me,
I thought I'd lost a friend.
See the mirror on the wall.
Forget the friend you've known.
You could be fairest of them all,
But you'll be alone.
Wicked queens and stepmothers
Turn mirrors into friends.
Let them have their mirror.
What I need is my friend.

When Kit finished, she stepped back a bit and waited a moment for the applause. Of all the contestants, Kit was receiving the most polite but also the least enthusiastic response.

Except from Phoebe. Tears were streaming down her face and she had given up all attempts to wipe them away. Instead, she was using her hands to applaud as loudly as she could. Kit had sacrificed winning the contest for their friendship. It meant everything to Phoebe.

As Kit stepped into the wings, Phoebe threw her arms around her. Then the two girls stood back just far enough so that they could see each other.

"It was so beautiful," Phoebe sighed, tears still coming down her face. "You're not sorry you gave up the dance routine?"

"First not-dumb thing I've done lately," Kit said. "And if you think you're leaving Plymouth forever, *you're* really dumb."

"But the house . . ."

"Grandma says to come stay with us," Kit said. "We want you here."

As the girls hugged again, Derek called all the contestants back onstage for the final judgment. Phoebe, standing happily beside Kit, realized that she wasn't caring about the moment she had dreaded most. Derek held up each contestant's right arm and waited for the audience to clap. As Derek held up Kit's arm, Phoebe clapped.

"You're not supposed to," Kit cautioned.

"I think you should win," Phoebe whispered.

"That's because you love really great poetry," Kit giggled.

"Attention! Attention!" Derek shouted, even though everyone was already paying attention to him. "The winner of the Plymouth Island Young People's Talent Contest is . . ."

12

MARGO MALLOY, our drum majorette!"
Derek said.

"Margo?" Phoebe gasped.

"Margo, my kid sister?" Kit asked.

"How could she?"

"How could *they*?" Kit whispered as she pointed to the audience.

Before Kit or Phoebe could do any more gasping, Mrs. Malloy had struck up the chords to "Hail, Plymouth Island." Herb was stepping onstage, planting a little tiara on Margo's head and handing her roses. Derek took her hand and led her down the runway. As she bowed to the audience, the audience rose to its feet, clapping and shouting "bravo" after "bravo" long after the song had ended. Derek stood back and let Margo stand alone at the end of the runway.

Margo took her final bows, and the curtain fell. The other contestants made their way to the stage door, with Derek and Herb and Mrs. Malloy right behind them. In a moment there was no one left backstage except Kit and Phoebe and Margo.

"It's over?" Margo asked. "That's it?"

"It wasn't enough?" Kit asked.

"I'm a star now," Margo declared. "Where did my public go?"

"Home," Phoebe said.

"Where we should all go," Kit added. "You were wonderful though. Congratulations."

"You deserved to win," Phoebe said.

"You two were good," Margo said. "But I guess no one can beat a drum majorette." She threw her baton in the air once more. As it came down, she reached out and grabbed it. She looked bewildered by her accomplishment. Then she put the baton under her arm and strutted out of the theater.

For the first time in a long time Phoebe

wasn't feeling anxious about being alone with Kit. She realized how much she had missed being Kit's best friend this summer. Maybe their differences weren't as important as the good feeling she felt now.

"You want to have a picnic at the tree house tomorrow?" Phoebe asked. "Just the two of us?"

"No fights? No feuds?"

"And definitely no majorettes. Just two old friends."

"You're a better friend to me than I knew, Kit."

"I can't stand it when you're mushy," Kit said. "It makes me mushy, too."

"But it's a tradition," Phoebe laughed. "We get mushy at the end of every summer."

The girls walked out the stage door. It was dark outside and the streetlights were on. Kit waved and walked across the parking lot to her grandmother's house. Phoebe saw Violet waiting for her outside the lobby.

"How about dinner down at the Sea Shanty?" Violet asked. "They're serving human beings and not just crabs, I hear. Besides, you deserve a night out to celebrate your performance. You were great, honey.

You deserved to win as far as I'm concerned."

"I'm not sure I didn't win," Phoebe beamed. "Kit and I are having a picnic tomorrow at the tree house."

"It was a beautiful poem," Violet said.

"Best I ever heard," Phoebe agreed. "And the day after tomorrow, when Mom and Dad get back to the island, I can tell them I had a great week after all. I never thought that would be possible."

"You and Kit friends again," Violet said, as the two of them walked toward the harbor under the September moon. "That makes for a nice ending to the summer, doesn't it?"

Phoebe nodded. "The *nicest* ending," she said. The nicest endings, she decided, weren't endings at all. They were really new beginnings.

Like this one.